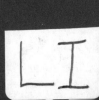

# The Granddaughter Necklace

# The Grand

BY SHARON DENNIS WYETH

ILLUSTRATED BY BAGRAM IBATOULLINE

 ARTHUR A. LEVINE BOOKS an imprint of Scholastic Inc.

daughter

Necklace

LIBRARY OF CONGRESS CATALOGING-IN-PUBLICATION DATA

Wyeth, Sharon Dennis.

The granddaughter necklace / Sharon Dennis Wyeth ; illustrations by Bagram Ibatoulline. — 1st ed.  p. cm.

Summary: A mother shares with her daughter stories of the generations of women in their family as each
individual has passed along the tales and a glittering necklace to her own daughter.

Includes notes on the author's exploration of her ancestry.

ISBN 978-0-545-08125-2 (hardcover : alk. paper) [1. Mothers and daughters–Fiction. 2. Necklaces–Fiction.
3. Storytelling–Fiction.]  I. Ibatoulline, Bagram, ill. II. Title.  PZ7.W9746Gr 2012   [Fic] –dc23   2011038933

10 9 8 7 6 5 4 3 2 1          13 14 15 16 17

First edition, January 2013

Printed in Singapore     46

The text was set in Berthold Baskerville Regular.
The display type was set in Bickham Script Pro Regular.
The art for this book was created using acryl-gouache.

Book design by Marijka Kostiw

FOR CAROLYN EDMONIA LEWIS COLEMAN,

MY AUNT AND CURRENT MATRIARCH, AND

FOR ROBIN RUE AND

ROSINA WILLIAMS WITH GRATITUDE

*—S. D. W.*

Once there was a girl named Frances, who took a boat across the sea. Her mother gave her a glittering necklace that would belong to me someday. Handed down through generations, it's a necklace worn by the women and girls in my family.

*When* I first saw the crystal beads, they hung on my own mother's neck. Nighttimes when she tucked me into bed, that necklace shone in the lamplight.

"I like that necklace, Mommy! Where did you get it?"

"This necklace belonged to your grandma and the other grandmas before her," she said.

My mother then began to tell me story after story, first about herself

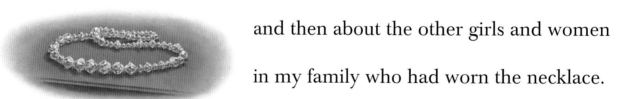

and then about the other girls and women in my family who had worn the necklace. Like the necklace, these stories had been handed down.

My mother's name is *Evon. . . .*

*When* Evon was a little girl, she loved to talk. She chatted with her friends in school instead of listening to the teacher. Her teacher sent a note home. Evon's mother wasn't pleased, but she wasn't harsh. "There are times you must keep quiet, dear," she said, "and times you must speak up."

Evon learned her lesson and listened to her teacher. But when the school put on a play, she spoke right up and got the leading part.

The play was based on *Cinderella.* Her mother made her a fancy ball gown. And so she'd feel like a real princess, Evon's mother gave her the glittering necklace.

"Good luck, sweetheart," she said.

Evon's mother's name was *Mildred. . . .*

*When* Mildred was a little girl, her house was in the mountains. But she left home when she was young to live with an aunt in a far-off town. Mildred's parents had thirteen children but her Aunt Stella had only one. In a home with fewer mouths to feed, Mildred would have more to eat. And Aunt Stella's little girl would have someone to play with. Besides, Aunt Stella was quite well-off, a seamstress.

*On* the day that Mildred left home, her whole family piled into the wagon with her. Her father drove the horses and her mother held her suitcase. The family rode across a bridge to a train station where the train tracks ran along a river. When she heard the train whistle, Mildred cried. It was time to say good-bye. Her mother was the one who hugged her hardest. Just as they were parting, she lifted the necklace off her neck and gave it to her daughter. "I love you, darling girl," she said.

"I love you too," said Mildred.

Mildred's mother's name was *Cordelia. . . .*

*When* Cordelia was a little girl, she had a glorious voice. Her favorite hymn was "His Eye Is on the Sparrow." Even though she was very young, at church on Sunday mornings she sang solos. And on Monday mornings, she helped with the wash. She and her mother carried the family's soiled clothes and sheets outside to the yard and tossed them into a metal tub filled with soap and boiling hot water. One time the water splashed too high and poor Cordelia's hand was burned.

Cordelia's mother rubbed the burn with aloe, but the hand was badly scarred. Cordelia was ashamed of how it looked and refused to leave the house, even for church. But then the special Sunday came when she would be baptized.

*Her* mother laid out a clean dress for her and her father polished her shoes. Her mother brushed her hair for her section by section until it was all curled. But when it was time to leave, Cordelia dragged her feet.

"If I go to be baptized, everyone will see the scar. The other girls and boys might call me ugly."

Cordelia's mother gently took her daughter's injured hand and placed the crystal necklace in her palm.

"That scar can't touch the beauty that's inside you, Cordelia. Wear these beads, my angel. Hold your head up high, and remember who you are."

Cordelia's mother's name was *Sallie*. . . .

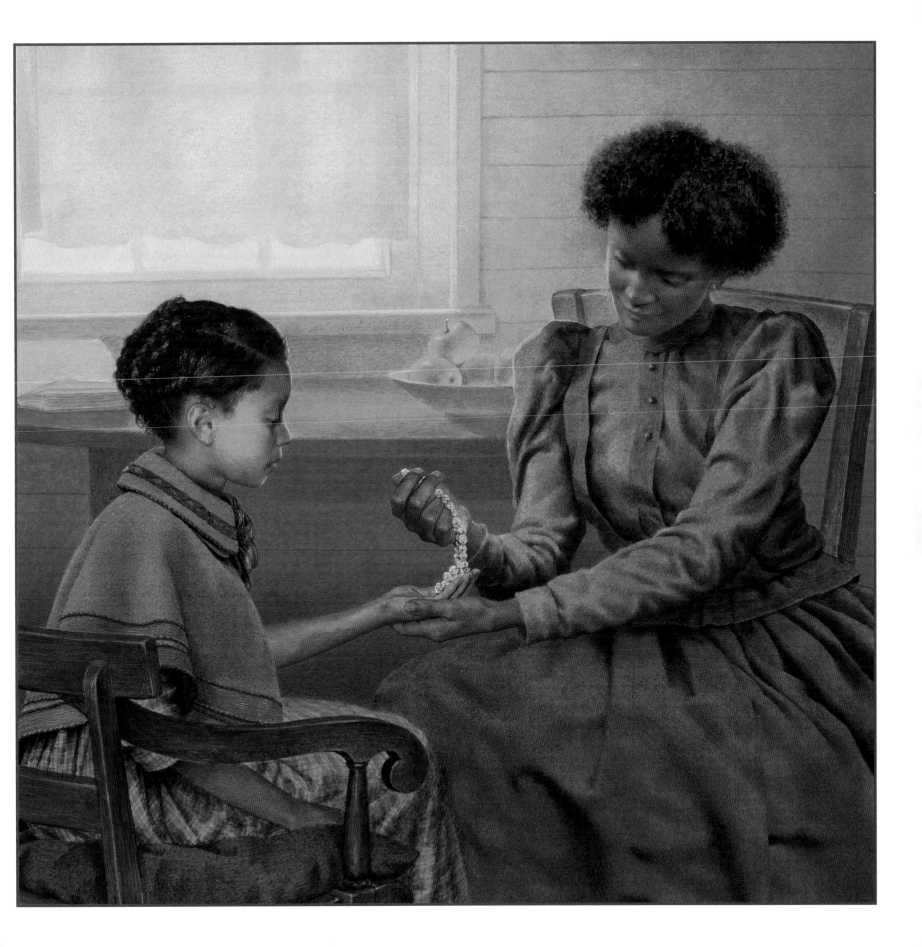

*When* Sallie was a little girl, she liked to bake. She got up early every day to help her ma make two dozen biscuits. The biscuits baked in a big, cast-iron stove. When they were done, Sallie's father ate three or four of them with eggs and homemade sausage. Sallie and her mother each could easily eat two, especially with fresh apple butter. As for the rest of the biscuits, they were left on the sill for lunch and supper.

But then a morning came when a hand reached through the window and a single biscuit disappeared from the plate. Sallie peeked outside. In the yard there was a hungry-looking man and his family. Offering him the plate, Sallie went to get the flour and began again to bake.

"After they've had their breakfast, they'll need more to eat," she told her mother and father.

"My girl sure can bake," boasted Sallie's father.

"What makes me glad," said Sallie's mother, "is her great big heart." She hung the beads 'round Sallie's neck.

Sallie's mother's name was *Frances. . . .*

*When* Frances was a little girl, she lived in Ireland. After she came to America, she wound up on a farm. They say she met an older gentleman named Theodore on a rainy road. He helped her up onto his horse and invited her to his home, a farmhouse on a hill where he lived all by himself. They became a family and had a girl named Sallie. They grew vegetables and flowers and raised chickens. They say that when folks stopped by their house, there was pound cake and an extra pipe, and that Frances was a good storyteller and that she spoke with a brogue.

As for the glittering necklace she once wore, it belongs to me now.

*It* happened on the day I turned sixteen. My mother, brothers, and I were leaving for my party. It should have been a happy day, but I was feeling sad.

"Why are you unhappy?" my mother asked.

I didn't want to say. But she guessed it was about my dad. Since my parents had gotten a divorce, I didn't see my father much. On my big day, he wouldn't be with me.

"If your dad could see you now, he'd be very proud," said Mom. We walked out to the car. "Happy birthday, Sugar," she said, tossing me the necklace.

I caught the beads in the air. "But that's yours," I said.

"I've worn it all these years," said my mother. "It's your turn now. After all, it's a granddaughter necklace."

"Why do you call it that?" I asked.

"Because everyone who wears it is somebody's granddaughter," she said with a laugh. As she fastened it around my neck, I lit up inside.

*I* am Sharon, daughter of Evon. Evon was the daughter of Mildred. Mildred was the daughter of Cordelia, who was the daughter of Sallie. Sallie was the daughter of Frances. And Frances was the daughter of a woman whose name I have not yet discovered. I wish I knew who she was.

I like to sing and cook. I grow roses in my garden. I write stories for a living and now I have my own daughter.

*My* girl, Georgia, plays catch with her dad after school

or goes for a ride on her bike. Sometimes we

bake an apple pie to pack up for a family hike.

But her favorite thing is music. She's quite good

at piano. In fact, tomorrow is her big recital. I know

that she'll be nervous, but she's also brave. I'll surprise her with the

granddaughter necklace after she's through playing.

"I'm proud of you," I'll tell her, "not just now, but every day.

This necklace says you're one of us . . .

*. . . and forever loved.*"